Nicole Estvanik

To Joyce H. Eisnor

April 24, 1990

THE SNOWMAN
WHO WANTED TO SEE JULY

Story by Nicole B. Estvanik
Illustrations by Benton Mahan

Raintree Publishers
Milwaukee

To my teacher, Mrs. Day,
who inspires me, and to my family,
who is always there for me.

—N.E.

To Anna, Megan, and Kailey.

—B.M.

1 2 3 4 5 6 7 8 9   93 92 91 90 89

Library of Congress Number: 89-10424

Library of Congress Cataloging-in-Publication Data

Estvanik, Nicole B.
   The snowman who wanted to see July.

   Summary: A young girl tries to fulfill the dream of a snowman to see July.
   1. Children's writings. [1. Snowmen—Fiction. 2. Children's writings]   I. Title.
PZ7.E82Sn   1989 [Fic]   89-10424
ISBN 0-8172-2779-2

There once was a snowman who wanted to see July. He should have been happy with his red scarf, his blue, woolly mittens, and his big, black top hat, but he longed to spy the butterflies hiding in the grass and to watch the flowers bloom.

Every year he'd shout, "I want to stay alive! I want to see July!" But each year he melted, and his raisin eyes were eaten by the birds.

Every winter when he was being built, he would call out to the little girl, "Help me! Build me so that I can see July!" But the little girl never seemed to hear him.

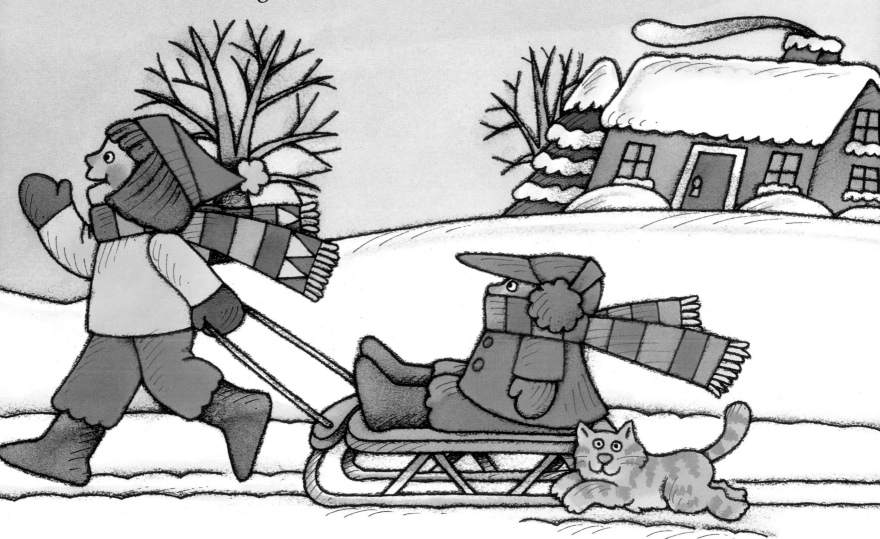

Finally one year the snowman couldn't stand it any longer. "That does it! I will see July this year. I must!" he declared. And true to his word, when the sun came out, he wouldn't melt.

9

Foolish snowman!" called the sun. "I will shine in your eyes and make them fall out. Then you won't see July." But the little girl heard the sun and put sunglasses on the snowman, and his eyes stayed in.

11

Well," said the sun, "I will shine on your nose, and it will shrink. Then your sunglasses won't stay on. Next I will shine in your eyes, and they will fall out, and you won't see July." But the little girl put suntan lotion on the snowman's nose, and his nose didn't shrink.

13

Well," said the sun, "I will heat this storm cloud and make it rain. The lotion will wash off, and your nose will shrink. Your sunglasses will fall off, and your eyes will fall out, and you won't see July." But the little girl held an umbrella over the snowman, and his lotion didn't wash off.

The sun told the rain to stop, hoping the umbrella would be taken down, but it wasn't. So the sun set to thinking very hard. Who ever heard of a snowman in July? Something had to be done. He called the wind. "Blow down that umbrella," he directed.

The wind blew with all his might, but the little girl held the umbrella, and he could not blow it from her hands. So the sun and the wind waited for her to tire of holding the umbrella. They waited for hours, and so did she. But finally she couldn't hold it any longer.

The sun smiled. But the smile soon turned to a frown when the little girl's brother came out with a hammer. Together the children nailed the umbrella down and then went inside for dinner. All during dinner, the little girl kept looking out the window to make sure the snowman was all right.

That night, as she lay in bed, she thought about the snowman. Quietly she got out of bed, tiptoed past her parents' bedroom, and ran down the stairs. Still wearing her slippers, the little girl slipped out into the dark night. She ran to the snowman and gave him a big kiss. "Good night," she whispered. She didn't see the snowman smile as she ran back into the house.

The next morning was bright and cheery. The little girl and her brother ran down the stairs. They ate a quick breakfast. Then, excitedly, the two raced off to tell their friends about the marvelous snowman. They came back with a group of children who wanted to see it for themselves. They were quite surprised and pleased.

He's going to see July," the little girl said. "He'll be famous!" cried one of the children. All of them edged closer to get a better look at the snowman. As they crowded around him, they began to joke and push. Suddenly, one of the children lost his balance and fell right into the snowman. The children cried in dismay as the snowman toppled to the ground and broke into a million pieces.

The little girl jumped forward. Blinking back tears, she grabbed the snow and tried to put the snowman back together. Seeing his chance, the sun came out and shone in all his brightness. Slowly, the snow melted, leaving the raisin eyes to be eaten by the birds. The snowman was gone.

The little girl's brother walked sadly away. Their friends left, too. But one stayed behind and put her arm around the little girl.

"You know," she said, "nature has a pattern that is very hard to break."

"But sometimes it doesn't hurt to try," the little girl thought, and she was right. Because of his ambition, the snowman had come closer to achieving his dream than ever before.

Nicole Beth Estvanik was born in Enfield, Connecticut, and has lived there all of her life, along with her parents and her sister, Lauren. Enfield, which is a town of 45,000 to 50,000 people, is just north of Hartford (and of Bristol, the hometown of another 1989 Publish-A-Book Contest winner).

At ten years old, Nicole has many interests. She enjoys crafts and likes to invent things. She collects stickers, postcards, and foreign money. Ballet and piano lessons also keep her busy, and she enjoys performing in the recitals. Reading and writing, of course, are also important to Nicole. In addition to stories, she has written plays and poems.

When not busy with these activities, Nicole attends Thomas Alcorn School. There, while in the fourth grade, she wrote *The Snowman Who Wanted to See July*. Although the story has much to do with magic, it is also a tale of characters trying to achieve the impossible. Nicole writes on this theme because she thinks it is important to reach for dreams.

Among her own dreams, Nicole would like to someday become a teacher. She plans to continue writing and hopes to be published again. As one of this year's grand-prize winners, Nicole—like the snowman in her story—seems to have taken a giant step toward achieving her dream.

The twenty honorable-mention winners in the **1989 Raintree Publish-A-Book Contest** were: Andy Binder, Rochester Hills, Michigan; Lauren Boyle, Melrose Park, Pennsylvania; Michael B. Cain, Annapolis, Maryland; Kristin Dehring, Bridgman, Michigan; Caitlin E. Foito, Bellevue, Washington; Emily Gilbert, Dayton, Ohio; Cameron Gordon, Harrisburg, Illinois; Jessica Gordon, Hidden Hills, California; JC Gossett, Roseland, New Jersey; Meghan Gurgol, Troy, Michigan; Andy Hoopes, Afton, Wyoming; Kelli Hutchinson, Faulkton, South Dakota; Amanda Michelle Lee, Lyons, Wisconsin; Christopher C. Martin, Woodward, Oklahoma; Anna Messick, Harrisburg, Pennsylvania; Nicholas Mey, Brighton, Michigan; Stephanie Potter, Plano, Texas; Jennifer Prestwood, Mary Esther, Florida; Joe Steed, Monmouth, Oregon; Nicholas Vogt, Lakeview, Arizona.

Benton Mahan lives on a small farm in central Ohio with his wife, Anna, and daughters, Megan and Kailey. He has been illustrating children's books for over fifteen years and teaches illustration at the Columbus College of Art and Design.